I'm Coming To Get You!

I'm

First published in the United States 1984 by
Dial Books for Young Readers
A Division of NAL Penguin Inc.
2 Park Avenue, New York, New York 10016

Published in Great Britain by Andersen Press Ltd.
Copyright © 1984 by Tony Ross /All rights reserved
Library of Congress Catalog Card Number: 84-5831
Printed in Hong Kong
First Pied Piper Printing 1987
C O B E
3 5 7 9 10 8 6 4 2

A Pied Piper Book is a registered trademark of
Dial Books for Young Readers,
a division of NAL Penguin Inc.,
® TM 1,163,686 and ® TM 1,054,312.

I'M COMING TO GET YOU!
is published in a hardcover edition by
Dial Books for Young Readers.
ISBN 0-8037-0434-8

Coming To Get You!

TONY ROSS

Dial Books for Young Readers · New York

a pied piper book

Deep in another galaxy a spaceship rushed toward

a tiny, peaceful planet.

It landed, and out jumped a loathsome monster.

"I'm coming to get you!" it howled.

The monster crushed all the gentle banana people.

It smashed their statues and scattered their books.

It chewed up the mountains

and drank the oceans. It had the jellyfish for dessert.

It gobbled up the whole planet except for…

the middle, which was too hot, and the ends,
which were too cold.

Still hungry, the monster flew off in his spaceship, nibbling small stars along the way.

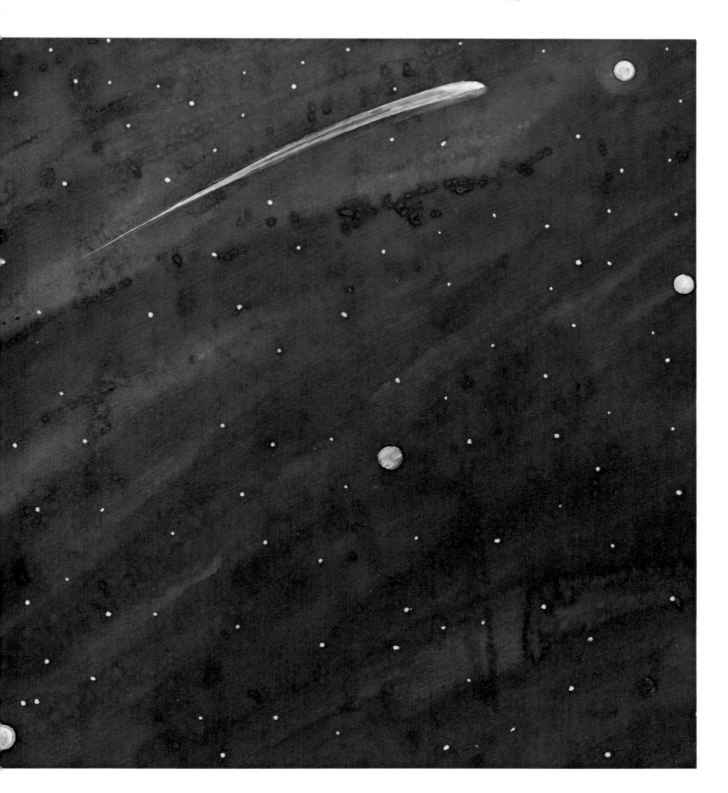

He had seen a pretty blue planet called Earth.

The monster found little Tommy Brown on its radar.
"I'm coming to get you!" it roared.

It was bedtime, and Tommy was listening to a story all about scary monsters.

The spaceship neared Earth, and the monster found out where Tommy lived.

It circled the town, looking for the right house.

As Tommy crept up to bed, he checked every stair for monsters.

He looked in every place they could hide.

Once he thought he heard a bump outside his window.

The monster hid behind a rock and waited for dawn.
"I'm coming to get you!" it hissed.

In the daylight Tommy felt silly for having been
so scared of monsters.

Then, with a terrible roar, the monster pounced....

But Tommy just walked right by.

TONY ROSS

is the prolific author and/or illustrator of over eighty books for children. He wrote *I'm Coming to Get You!*, his first book for Dial, for his then three-year-old daughter, who was afraid of monsters, to show her that "monsters may seem scary at first, but really they're nothing at all."

Mr. Ross is known throughout the world for his delightfully wacky retellings of traditional folk and fairy tales. Some of them include *Foxy Fables*, *The Boy Who Cried Wolf*, *Lazy Jack*, and *Stone Soup*, all recently published by Dial. An avid collector of model tin soldiers, Mr. Ross lives with his wife and daughter in Anglesey, Wales.